Sunny Bunny
Loves His Dad

by Penny Little
illustrated by Sean Ju

Sandy Creek

Sunny Bunny was born
on a long hot midsummer's day,
and how he loved the bright yellow sun!
Every day at sunrise he would race down
to the meadow to play,

and every evening at sunset,
Sunny Bunny would always be the last to go home.

But one day Sunny Bunny woke up
and the sun wasn't there. "Brrrr." He shivered,
looking up at the cold, gray, empty sky.
"Where can it have gone?"

Sunny Bunny waited all day for the sun to come out . . .
but it never did.

By snack time he was feeling very worried,
so he went to find his friends.

Little mouse was busy
collecting leaves and moss.
"The sun has gone missing,"
said Sunny Bunny.
"Can you help me find it?"

"Very sorry, Sunny Bunny," she said, "but I've got my nest to build. Why don't you give me a hand?" But Sunny Bunny didn't feel like building a nest, he felt too sad.

"Come and have a nut fight," squealed the squirrels,
grabbing handfuls of hazelnuts.
"Have you seen the sun?" asked Sunny Bunny.
"I don't feel like playing today."

But the squirrels just shook their bushy tails and laughed.
"Ouch!" A flying hazelnut hit Sunny Bunny right on the nose.

He felt even more sad.

Sunny Bunny went home to his burrow. He hid under
his favorite blanket and hugged his favorite toy.
Where had the sun gone?
When would it come out to play again?

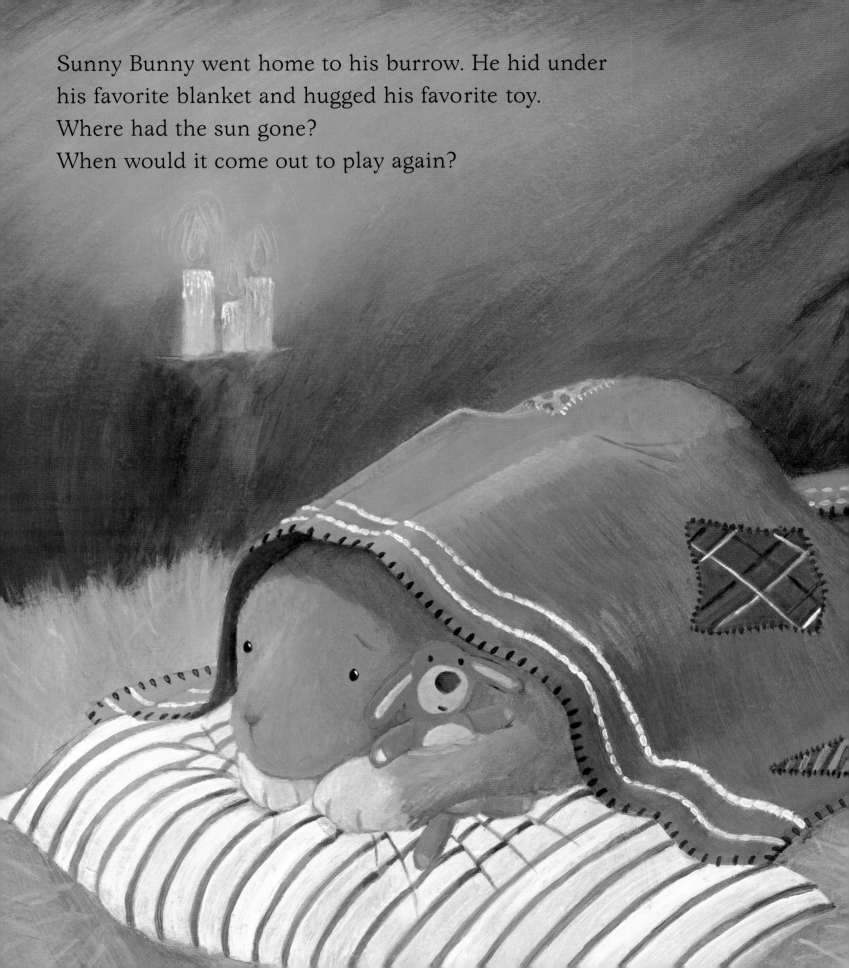

"Do you know where the sun is?"
Sunny Bunny asked Dad, at bed time.

"The sun is never far away," smiled Dad, tucking him into his cozy bed. "It's only playing hide-and-seek in the clouds. Now go to sleep, my Sunny Bunny. Everything will be better in the morning."

But Sunny Bunny couldn't sleep.
He tried and tried but it was no good.

All night long he lay awake in his burrow,
worrying about the sun.

Then he remembered what his dad had told him.
If the sun is playing hide-and-seek, he thought,
then I must go and find it!

He peeped out.
In the distance he could see a pale pink patch of sky.
Was it the sun? Was that where it was hiding?
Without another thought he set off to see.

Down in the cold dark woods a little bottom
was sticking up out of the ground, and dirt was
flying everywhere. "Excuse me," shouted Sunny Bunny.
"Have you seen the sun?"

Baby Badger unplugged his stripy head. "Have I seen the what?" he said.
"The sun," said Sunny Bunny. "It's warm, glowy and makes everyone happy."
"Hmmm," said Baby Badger, "I don't think so, but ask the baby owls.
They can see a l . . . o . . . n . . . g way away."

High in the trees the baby owls sat in a fluffy little row.
"Can you see the sun up there?" called Sunny Bunny.
"WhOO-oo-Oo needs the sun," they hooted happily,
"when you can have the bright silver mOOO-oo-oOn!"

"The moon *is* beautiful,"
said Sunny Bunny.

"But not as beautiful as the
glorious golden sun," said another voice.

"My daddy!" shouted Sunny Bunny, running and jumping into his arms. "Where have you been?" asked Dad. "I've been playing hide-and-seek with the sun," said Sunny Bunny. "But it's just *too* clever at hiding," he added sadly.

Dad glanced up at the sky. "Not every day can be a sunny day, Sunny Bunny," he said, "but even when it's gloomy and grey and the sun is hiding, remember that it is always there. And that it will always come back."

"Now, come with me," he smiled.
"I have a feeling something exciting is going to happen."

Together they climbed the hill, and suddenly
Sunny Bunny could see that the sky wasn't just pink any more,
it was red

and orange

and purple

and violet

and indigo all at once!

Below them, a shimmery sliver of fiery gold

peeped over the edge of the earth.

"Look, Dad!

LOOK!"

And together they laughed and danced
all the way home, in the glorious golden sunrise!

"We found it," shouted Sunny Bunny.
"We found the sun!"

For my lovely Eleanor – PL

For my Grandmas, who showed me the wonderful world
of scones and lemon curd tarts. – SJ

Text © 2010 by Penny Little
Illustrations © 2010 by Sean Julian

This 2010 edition published by Sandy Creek
by arrangement with Random House Children's Books

Sandy Creek
122 Fifth Avenue
New York, NY 10011

ISBN: 978-1-4351-2497-4

Printed and bound in China

1   3   5   7   9   10   8   6   4   2